Ghost Ship

CHRISTOPHER STITT

Illustrated by Jan D'Silva

sundance™

A Haights Cross Communications ® Company

The Characters

Toby

Isabella

Grandad

The Story Setting

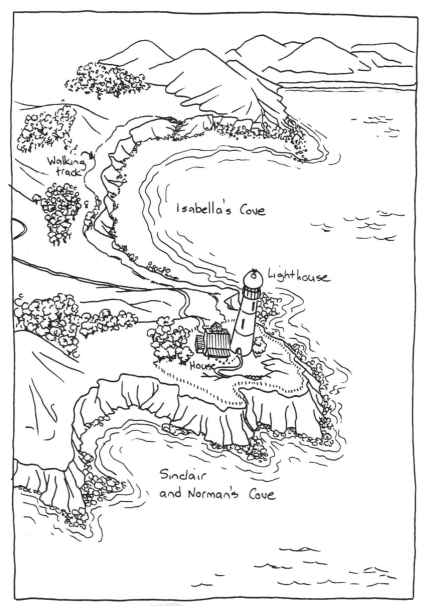

Walking track

Isabella's Cove

Lighthouse

House

Sinclair and Norman's Cove

TABLE OF CONTENTS

Chapter 1

Chapter 2

Chapter 3

A Ship Out to Sea

Toby stood on the cliffs with his grandad, looking out over the crashing sea.

"Looks like we're in for a storm," said Grandad. "I'd better go turn on the light in the lighthouse."

Toby loved spending his school vacations with his grandparents. They were lighthouse keepers.

Toby breathed in the wet, salty air. "You can smell a storm, can't you?"

"Sure can. You take after your old grandad." He put his hand on Toby's shoulder. "Are you coming to help turn on the light?"

"In a minute," Toby said as he watched his grandad head for the lighthouse.

Standing alone on the cliff, Toby could feel the wind blowing his hair. The salty air made his face tingle. He watched the seagulls ride the wind, just gliding.

Toby noticed something out at sea. It was
an old-fashioned ship, with sails and
rigging. It was kind of hazy and hard to
see. It was almost as if he could see
through it! "I'll have to tell Grandad.
Maybe I can get a better look through
the telescope," he said to himself.

Toby ran to the lighthouse and up the 135 steps. "There's a ship out there!" gasped Toby. "I need the telescope."

"Who could it be?" wondered Grandad.

Toby pointed the telescope at the exact place where he had seen the ship, but it had disappeared.

"It's gone, but I'm sure I saw it. It was an old ship, with sails and everything."

"The storm must be playing tricks on your eyes, Toby. There are no sailing ships in these parts."

Toby went to the window. He put his face against the glass as the rain poured down. It was impossible to see anything.

Thunder crashed above them as Toby and Grandad walked down the stairs.

"I'm sure I saw a ship," said Toby.

"Maybe you did," Grandad answered as he held the railing tightly. "Maybe it was a replica of an old ship. They make them for sight-seeing tours."

When they reached the house, Toby's grandmother was making supper. The warmth of the fire filled the room.

"That smells great, Grandma," Toby said as he rubbed his stomach.

He and Grandad sat at the table. Grandma served the steaming soup.

After supper, Toby went into the study. He remembered seeing a special book about old ships there.

Grandad found Toby studying the book when he walked in. Toby pointed to a picture in the book and said, "This looks just like the ship I saw."

14

The ship in the picture was amazing.
It was an old wooden ship with three
masts. Its sails were billowing in the wind.

Grandad looked at the picture. "The
Isabella. Lost at sea, October 12, 1892,"
he read. "What a beautiful ship."

"Lost at sea," repeated Toby. "That means it sank, and no one knows where. I couldn't have seen that ship."

"Maybe it was a ghost ship," Grandad said, as he ruffled Toby's hair.

As Toby fell asleep that night, his head was filled with thoughts of ghost ships. He was determined to solve the mystery of the missing ship, the *Isabella*.

CHAPTER 2

Shipwreck

The storm continued the next day.
Toby used the Internet to search for
information on shipwrecks. Finally, he
found a site that had information about
the *Isabella*.

"They think it vanished around here,"
said Toby excitedly.

"That must be a mistake," said Grandad. "According to the records, there haven't been any shipwrecks around here since the lighthouse was built."

Toby scrolled down the Web page. "Captain Stewart built the ship, and he named it after his daughter, Isabella."

"What did it carry?" asked Grandad.

"It was made to carry supplies, but it sank on its first trip. The only thing it was carrying was Stewart's family."

"Does it say anything about a search or the lighthouse?" asked Grandad.

Toby continued reading. "The lighthouse keeper said he never saw the ship. So they had no idea where to search."

Grandad looked sad. "What a tragedy. That happened a lot back then. It could have been lost anywhere along the coast."

21

After lunch, the rain finally stopped. Grandad was going to do a check on the lighthouse. "Toby, do you want to go with me?"

"No, thanks. I'm going to the cove to see if I can find anything interesting." Toby grabbed his coat from Grandma.

Toby went down the stairs to the beach.
He looked out across the sea. It was so
calm compared to the day before.
Suddenly, Toby tripped over something
and fell face-first into the sand.

Toby spit sand out of his mouth. Then he looked to see what had tripped him.

It was just a piece of wood, but something underneath it caught his eye. He dug deeper and discovered a bell. Toby carefully scraped off the barnacles and found a date carved on the side.

"1892," Toby read. He knew it could be the bell from the *Isabella*. He couldn't wait to show Grandad.

As Toby turned to leave, he heard someone crying. He stopped and listened. Where was the crying coming from?

CHAPTER 3

Isabella's Cove

Toby scanned the beach. He thought he was alone, until he saw a woman sitting on a rock. She was dressed like someone in a history book. Toby called to her, "Are you all right?"

The woman looked up and wiped her eyes. As Toby walked toward her, he realized that he could see right through her, just like the ship last night.

"You're a . . . a . . . ghost!" he gasped.

She sighed. "Yes, I am. I am Isabella."

"Are you Captain Stewart's daughter?"

Isabella stood up. "You know my father?"

"I found out about him and his ship, the *Isabella*, on the Internet," said Toby.

Isabella gave Toby a strange look. "Internet? What is that? A book?"

"No," Toby laughed. "But don't worry about it. It's too hard to explain."

"Is this the bell from the *Isabella*?" asked Toby. "Did the ship sink close to here?"

"Out there," sobbed Isabella as she pointed out to sea. "There was a terrible storm, and we didn't see the rocks. I was washed overboard. I drowned trying to swim to shore. I've been here ever since."

29

"Wasn't there a light on at the lighthouse?" Toby asked, pointing to the cliff.

"Light?" said Isabella. "We saw no light."

Toby was shocked. The lighthouse keeper's records showed that the light was on. Yet Isabella was saying it wasn't.

"Something's not right," said Toby. "Wait here while I go and see my grandfather."

Isabella curtsied. "Please help me. I've been here for so long. I can't stand it."

Toby put the bell under his arm and ran up the stairs toward the lighthouse.

"Grandad!" shouted Toby. "Look what I found." He handed Grandad the bell.

Grandad looked closely at the bell. "1892. Where did you find this?"

"On the beach. It's from the *Isabella*."

Toby wanted to tell Grandad about the ghost, but he didn't think he'd believe it.

"The *Isabella* was brand new in 1892," said Toby. "She was on her first voyage when she sank near here. Are you sure the light was on that night?"

Grandad got the old lighthouse logbook
from 1892. "Here it is. October 12.
Buddy, the lighthouse keeper, wrote
that no ships passed that night."

Toby looked at the entry. Someone was
lying. It had to be Buddy. Why would a
ghost lie?

"Does Buddy live in town?" asked Toby.

Grandad laughed. "In the cemetery.
He'd be well over 100 years old now. But
his great-grandson, Felix, lives nearby."

Toby grabbed the bell. "Where does he
live?"

"26 Blackburn Road." Grandad looked at
Toby. "Why do you want to know?"

"I need to see him. Something's wrong."

CHAPTER 4

A Cover-up?

Toby knocked on the door of the old cottage. A man opened the door.

"Hi. My name is Toby. My grandad is the lighthouse keeper. Are you Felix?"

Felix nodded and opened the door wider.

"Do you know anything about the *Isabella*?" Toby asked.

Felix's face looked grim. "I know nothing about it. Leave me alone." The door closed.

"He knows something," said Toby to himself. "I need to find out more."

Toby got back on the Internet to find out more about ghosts. Why was Isabella still in the cove? Why was the ghost ship still haunting the bay? It didn't take long for Toby to find what he needed.

He ran back down to the beach, where Isabella was waiting.

"Isabella," called Toby, "are you sure there was no light on that night?"

"Yes, I'm sure," said Isabella.

"I know why you're here," said Toby. "You're trapped. It happens when someone's death is a mystery. I was sent to find you and solve the mystery."

"If you solve it, I'll get to see my true love again," she sighed. "My Sinclair."

"Come for a walk," said Toby as he headed toward the edge of the cove.

"I can't go," Isabella cried. "I've tried."

"I'm going to look for more wreckage," said Toby. "I won't be long."

Toby crossed the rocks into the next cove. He didn't find any more wreckage, but he did hear someone shouting.

"Captain. Captain Stewart. We're here."

Toby saw a man dressed in ragged clothes, calling out to the ghost ship. He was see-through like Isabella.

"Are you Sinclair?" shouted Toby.

"You can see me? Who are you? How do you know Sinclair?"

Toby approached the man. "I know Isabella. I'm trying to find out what happened the night the ship sank."

"Isabella," gasped the man. He turned and looked down the beach. "Master Sinclair," he called. "Master Sinclair."

A well-dressed man appeared. "What is it, Norman?"

Norman pointed to Toby. "This boy knows Isabella."

"Is she a ghost, too?" asked Sinclair.

Toby nodded. "She's trapped in the next cove."

"You must help us. I haven't seen my Isabella since I dived overboard that night to save her," explained Sinclair. "I begged Norman to help me, too."

Norman put his hand through his chest. "As you can see, we didn't make it."

Sinclair sighed, "My dear Isabella."

"I can help you," said Toby, "if I solve the mystery of why the ship went down. Was the lighthouse working that night?"

"No," answered Norman. "If there had been a light, we'd still be flesh and blood."

"Not quite," said Toby. "You'd be over 100 years old!"

"We have lost track of time. You're the only person to actually see us in all these years."

Sinclair snapped his fingers. "This boy is the one who can save us from haunting this beach forever."

CHAPTER 5

A Forgery

Sinclair asked Toby what clues he had. Toby told the ghosts everything he knew.

"The logbook says there was a light on?" asked Norman. "I swear I didn't see it."

Sinclair shook his fists. "There was no light. The record must be wrong."

"That's what I thought," agreed Toby.
"I can't prove it, though."

"Toby! Toby!" called Grandad.

"That's my grandfather. I'd better go."

"Please save us," pleaded Sinclair.
"I can't go on without my Isabella."

Toby ran off down the beach. "I'll do my best. Don't give up hope."

Toby met his grandad in Isabella's cove. She was standing next to Grandad, but he had no idea that a ghost was there.

"You have a visitor at the lighthouse," said Grandad.

"A visitor?" asked Toby.

"I think you'll find it very interesting, Sherlock," answered Grandad.

Grandma was serving cookies and tea when Toby and his grandad walked in.

Felix was waiting for Toby. "I'm sorry I was so rude," he apologized. Then he handed a black book to Grandad. "This is my great-grandfather's diary. It tells all about the night of October 12, 1892."

Toby was surprised and excited. "What happened?"

Grandad opened the diary and read. "It has been a bad week. Storm after storm. I was so tired that I fell asleep on my watch. The light must have gone out."

"So that's how it happened." Toby was amazed. He had been right.

"I didn't know anything had gone wrong," Grandad read. "Then I heard that the *Isabella* was missing in my waters. So I lied in the logbook."

Toby looked over at Felix. He could see
the sadness in the man's eyes. Toby felt
sorry for him, but even more sorry for
the people on the ship who had lost
their lives. They had haunted the cove
for over 100 years.

"My great-grandfather lived with the guilt
for the rest of his life," said Felix.

Toby was still thinking about the stranded ghosts. "We need to tell someone that the ship must have sunk out in the bay."

Felix looked at Toby. "I'm sure the museum would like to know."

"I mean the families of the people on the ship," said Toby. "They'll finally know what happened to their relatives."

CHAPTER 6

Bon Voyage

Toby returned to the beach the next day. He found Isabella in Sinclair's arms.

"You're all in the same cove!" said Toby. "I solved the mystery!"

"We're free!" Norman danced around the beach. "We wanted to wait to tell you."

Isabella kissed Toby. "We want to thank you for our freedom."

Toby felt his face turn red. "It was nothing. The old lighthouse keeper's great-grandson had his diary. It told how the light went out the night the *Isabella* sank."

"I knew there was no light," announced
Norman, "as sure as I'm a ghost."

"What will happen now?" asked Sinclair.

Toby pointed to some men on the stairs.
"Your relatives were told what happened.
They want divers to look for the wreck.
Then they'll put it in the local museum."

The ghost ship, the *Isabella,* sailed into view again. It was an awesome sight.

"That's our ride home," said Norman. "We'll miss this place. Well, only a little."

"Climb aboard," the captain called from the ship. "I'm glad to see you all again. I've been sailing these waters for years."

Captain Stewart winked at Toby. "Thank
you, young man. You did a wonderful
thing."

Isabella, Sinclair, and Norman swam out to
the ship. The captain helped them aboard.

Toby waved as the ship disappeared over the horizon.

"Goodbye! Good luck!" he called.

"Who are you waving to?" Grandad asked as he came up behind Toby.

"Just some old friends."

GLOSSARY

barnacles
small shells
attached to rocks

billowing
moving about
in the wind

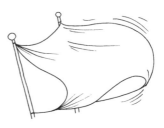

cove
a small sheltered
area of beach

curtsied
bowed

hazy

misty and foggy

replica

a true-to-life copy

rigging

ropes and chains that
work the sails and mast

scanned

looked at quickly

Talking with the Author and the Illustrator

Christopher Stitt (author)

What do you keep under your bed?
All sorts of junk that I don't use much because I'm too scared to go under there!

What are you most scared of?
Big dogs!

Jan D'Silva (illustrator)

What day of the year do you like best?
The first day of any vacation.

What do you keep under your bed?
Dust and the dust monster.

What are you most scared of?
The dust monster.

A Haights Cross Communications ✦ Company

Copyright © 2003 Sundance/Newbridge Educational Publishing, LLC

Published by Sundance Publishing
P.O. Box 740, One Beeman Road, Northborough, MA 01532
800-343-8204

Copyright © text Christopher Stitt
Copyright © illustrations Jan D'Silva

First published 2000 as Sparklers by
Blake Education, Locked Bag 2022, Glebe 2037, Australia
Exclusive United States Distribution: Sundance Publishing

ISBN-13: 978-0-7608-6975-8
ISBN-10: 0-7608-6975-8

Printed in China